BOOK ONE-THE EX LOVER

Chapter One

England 1817

William kissed my neck and pushed me down on the bed seconds after we'd arrived in our room. I was in no mood for anything in the least sexual, or even romantic for that matter, but let him continue anyway. He tugged at the top bow on my bodice.

"Damn and blast, never did like these things," he said.

He gave up trying and instead chose to squeeze my breast through the thick material of my dress.

"William, I know tonight's events have unsettled you, so I think we should talk about our dilemma."

"You're right, my darling."

He flopped over onto his back and looked up at the canopy above our bed. I rolled onto my side, and set my head upon his shoulder.

He took my hand and rubbed the back of it before setting its palm flat upon his chest, covering it with his own.

"I think we need to get you pregnant," he said.

No, surely he could not mean that.

I turned my head away unable to look him in the eye. Not that I didn't secretly wish for a child, but I wanted our offspring to belong to him, and we both knew that was impossible.

"Look at me, my darling girl."

I refused to. My focus remained on the wall opposite our bed.

"Gillian, please, you were right; we have to talk about this matter."

Why did this have to happen to us when we'd been so happy and content for years?

Turning my head slowly to face him, I knew he'd see tears forming in my eyes, and that would make him sad.

"Damn my brother. Why after all these years of avoiding marriage has he chosen now to become betrothed? He is forty and four and, I assumed, a lifelong bachelor," said William.

I took comfort by snuggling into my husband's shoulder knowing we shouldn't begrudge his brother's happiness, but our almost perfect world was crumbling apart because of it.

With Nigel's upcoming marriage to Felicity there would most likely be a child, an heir to the name and estate. William and I being childless could quite well end up with nothing, not even a roof over our heads, once his mother passed away.

"Let me at least take some comfort in your body tonight," he whispered.

I could not deny him pleasure. He deserved it. I opened my bodice and petticoat for him.

He kissed the top of my head before circling my nipple with his finger. My pussy pulled, my womb tightened, and then he leaned over to kiss me. How I wished things could be different for us.

I ran my hand through his thick dark hair. We had planned to begin filling the nursery as soon as we were married, but then William had been persuaded by his best friend to travel to India. The adventure of a lifetime, he'd called it. He'd asked me to go along, but my sister was with child at the time and I'd wanted to assist her at the birth, so I had declined.

While in India, William had caught a dreadful tropical fever, and he had fallen ill two weeks after arriving back in England. The doctors didn't think he would survive, and I had assumed I would be a widow. He'd shivered continuously despite the sweat covering his body and face. They'd placed him in a bath of ice water hoping to bring down his temperature, but he'd grown delirious and drifted in and out of consciousness for three days. However, a day later his fever broke and he was able to speak. A month later he looked like his old self again, eating, walking and riding his horse as if nothing had been wrong with him. However, the lasting effect of whatever had ailed him reared its ugly head in the bedroom a few weeks later.

"Come here, my darling. I have waited months to make love to you. You must be as needy as I am."

He had undressed me. I had stood naked before him. William had sucked my nipples, run his hand down my belly, spread my legs, and taken delight in plunging his tongue into my pussy. Being the eager lover that I am, I had pulled at his pants only to discover that his cock was still flaccid. I took it in my hand, caressing it, thinking that perhaps it was my fault and that my body no longer excited him. No matter how many times I rubbed my hand over his shaft it remained limp on his thighs.

"William, don't you love me any more?" I'd cried and flopped face-down on the bed, wondering if he'd taken a lover while in India.

William had grabbed me, scooped me up in his arms, and turned me around to face him.

"I will always love you."

"But I don't excite you now."

"You thrill me in more ways than you can ever imagine."

"But your cock."

He nodded. "I can't seem to feel anything down there like I used to, but it's nothing to do with you or your body."

We'd thought his problem would pass, but every time we attempted to make love things became more frustrating for us.

"Damn, what is wrong with me?"

One night William had tried masturbating, but still his cock hung limp and lifeless. He'd walked away from the bed and thrown a glass against the wall. He'd tried to penetrate me for an hour and it had taken its toll on both of us. He'd experienced some hardness but not enough to slide inside my pussy with any success. On his last attempt I had burst into tears because I'd never seen my husband in such a desperate-looking state before.

"Gillian, do not cry, do not cry. I'm sure everything will be all right for us." He'd leaned against the mantelpiece in our room, his head down on his arm, as he'd spoken those words. I could hear his voice was weak, almost as if he was on the brink of tears too.

That had been two years ago. We had accepted that the fever had left him impotent. His mother has been anxious for an heir from the moment we had married. William, being the gentleman that he is, wanted to tell her and the rest of the family that he was to blame for the empty nursery. However, I knew how humiliating it was for him, for any man, so I'd forced him to go along with the story that it was I who had the problem conceiving. My mother-in-law has accepted that I am barren and sometimes cannot bear to look at me. And, of course, it has been two and a half years since I've had the pleasure of a cock inside me. William has since found other ways to bring me to orgasm, but I haven't had the courage to tell him that my climaxes have never been the same as before his fever. And now, tonight, his brother Nigel announced his upcoming marriage to Felicity. She is young and will no doubt now bear the first Langtry heir.

William fingered my breasts once again. I closed my eyes, feeling his hand move down my belly, sinking lower into my curls.

"Spread your legs for me."

My heart beat faster. I had mixed emotions. I always do at this point. I longed for my husband to touch my clit, to finger fuck me, but regretted that he can't be inside me and therefore would experience no pleasure of his own.

I spread my legs as he requested. Soon he was rubbing my clit until it was swollen and ached for more. He kissed me as he always does when he knows that I'm about to reach my climax. Covering my mouth with his, his tongue flicked along my lower lip. That night I almost bit it when he pressed hard on my nub and took me over the edge. He nuzzled my cheek with his nose, as his finger made a trail around my folds. He took some of my juices on his thumb and twirled them around. A warmth spread throughout my pussy and womb as he inserted two fingers inside me.

He is an expert at this now. He knows exactly what I like; how long it takes me to come, and can even tell when I'm moments away from finding paradise. I shifted my ass and raised my hips to meet with his thrusts. That night I came quickly, whimpering into his shoulder as I found release.

"You know you will have to make love with another man to conceive the child we need." I looked him in the eye and knew that he meant what he'd just told me.

"William, no, I could not do that to you and…" I could not imagine myself with another man, being intimate with someone other than my husband. Not after all the years we'd been together.

He put his hand over my mouth to stop me from protesting further.

"We will make it as exciting an experience for you as we can. You deserve that. Not only have you been without my cock inside you for years, but you will have to bear the pains of childbirth, so a sexual adventure will be your reward."

"But what if this man ever told others that he had sex with me and fathered the child?"

"Yes, that could be a problem. A man blabbering his mouth off in our social circles, telling everyone that he fucked the delightful Lady Langtry, with her husband's permission no less, and got her in the family way." He smiled and tapped me on the nose.

"Would you not be jealous of another man being inside me?"

"Of course, my darling, but it will be such an experience for you, so I would be happy."

"William…"

"I have the solution. You will have sex with three men and none of them, nor we, will ever know which one actually fathered the child."

"Three men? William…I…"

"My dear, can you imagine how many orgasms you will enjoy? I will choose the men wisely, and it will be my gift to you, as I won't reveal who these men are until you meet them Yes, three men, three different sexual encounters."

Chapter Two

William was gone most of the week. On several occasions he'd returned home with quite the smile on his face.

"And what have you been up to, my dear husband?" I wrapped my arms around his body and set my head on his chest.

"It's a secret, but let me just say you are in for a wonderful time."

"Can you give me just a little clue?"

He pulled away from me and smiled. "Then that would ruin the surprise for you. However, I will just say two of the men have been selected. They are perfect, and both eagerly await the pleasure of your body. In fact, I had no problem whatsoever talking them into doing this for us. Once they knew their cocks would be buried deep inside your pussy they eagerly volunteered. Ah now, my darling, you are blushing. Surely you must know how delightful your body is?"

"And what about the third man?"

"I will be visiting him tomorrow, but I suspect he will also jump at the chance to ravish you, my dear."

* * * * *

It had all been finalized. William spent the following day securing the services of the last man.

I tossed and turned in bed, not sure if this was such a wise idea. My restlessness woke William in the middle of the night.

"Whatever is wrong? You're not coming down with something, are you?"

"I can't sleep because I don't think I can go through with this. You are the only man I've ever been intimate with."

"Look at it as a necessary thing that must be done to ensure our future. And you have always enjoyed pleasures of the flesh, have you not?"

It was true. I couldn't deny that. Since my wedding night I have enjoyed making love.

I nodded.

"Well then, you will have fun."

"But what about you?"

"My enjoyment will come from knowing you are being pleasured."

He lifted my hand and kissed the back of it.

"And these men, do they know that they will possibly father a child in the process of making love to me?"

"All three are more than happy to oblige us. Like I said, all three are eager to fuck you. I'm sure every man in a twenty-mile range of our house would love the opportunity to be inside that tight little quim of yours."

I swallowed, feeling my face flush. "May I please know who they are?"

He put his finger over my lips. "That is to be part of the allure and surprise. Only I know who they are, and that's how it will remain."

I swallowed. What if I did not like them…did not find them attractive? No, my husband would not do that to me. I was sure they were dashing and handsome, good lovers, and I would indeed find pleasure in their bodies.

He tapped me on the nose. "Now get a good night's sleep, for tomorrow morning your sexual adventures begin."

* * * * *

I wasn't sure why I'd chosen to put on one of my best dresses. After all, I was a married woman, and my liaison with this man was to be a one-time meeting.

"The carriage is ready and waiting," announced William.

My stomach flipped and bile rose in my throat. I stood but my legs shook. William walked over and drew me in close to him.

"My love, you are shaking."

"I'm petrified. After all, I'm not that experienced."

"And all the more reason for you to venture into other lands…so to speak."

He kissed me.

"And what if I enjoy this a little too much and become spoiled?"

"I give you full permission to enjoy each and every one of your orgasms. And if you feel like sucking a cock you also have my blessing. I'd hate my training to go to waste." He kissed the backs of both my hands. "Now let me escort you to the carriage."

My mother-in-law walked out of the drawing room as we headed to the front door.

"Mother, Gillian's going to visit a friend who is quite sick, which means I will be on my own today, so perhaps you and I can enjoy a game of cards."

"That would be splendid, and later Felicity will be visiting and has promised to play for us. I hear the girl is very talented on the harpsichord."

She glared at me. I do not play, I do not sew, and I do not bear children, none of the things a young lady and wife are supposed to do. A mother-in-law's worst nightmare for her son.

I took a deep breath. Perhaps a pregnancy would put me in a better light with her. William held my arm as we headed down the steps to where the driver opened the carriage door for me. William helped me up and I sat. Then he climbed in beside me and pulled out a scarf.

"I will blindfold you for your journey; that way when you arrive at your destination it will be a total surprise for you."

"So I know this house and this man?"

"Oh yes, and I hope it makes you happy. He has arranged to greet you in the carriage, so when you arrive you're to remain seated and blindfolded until he comes out to escort you inside."

Suddenly the whole thing sounded naughty, thrilling almost.

"Now I will bid you farewell and can't wait to see you later this evening."

He kissed me and wrapped the cloth around my eyes, and I was cast into darkness. The carriage rose up on one side, and I knew he'd left and that I was now alone. It jerked forward on its journey, and I rubbed my hands up my arms to try and keep warm. I listened for any little sound that would perhaps tell me where I was heading.

Birds sang out in a noisy chorus, the horses' hooves beat against the gravel on the road…and then came the sound of water. I heard a stream running close to the carriage. I settled back, now wondering who would climb into the coach when it reached its destination. A cool breeze hit my cheek, and I sensed we'd turned into another direction. We continued for five more minutes along a path where I heard the leaves rustling in the breeze. The carriage stopped, and I held my breath. My heart beat so fast that I could hear it playing like drums in my head and ears. There was stillness, now, an almost eerie silence as I waited. I swallowed, almost tempted to take off my blindfold, or at least lift it slightly so I could see where I was, and perhaps it would give me a clue as to the identity of gentleman number one. But that would be cheating, and yes, spoil the fun that William had planned for me. The wait was killing me. I began tapping my feet when at last I felt a breeze on my arm. Shortly after, warmth penetrated my left thigh and I knew someone was now sitting on the seat beside me.

"Gillian," a man's voice whispered into my ear.

No, surely it could not be.

I recognized the deep timber of his voice. It was so distinctive, and even with just one word escaping his mouth I knew who he was. Not only did my heart flutter, but my pussy clenched and pulled as I realized who my first lover would be.

"Andrew," I whispered back.

He kissed my cheek. "Yes, dearest Gillian, it's me."

Andrew ran his hand over the back of mine, sending shivers down my back and legs. I closed my eyes even though blindfolded. Had it not been that my parents had insisted on a match with a titled gentleman such as William, I would have married Andrew Hathaway. William is quite aware of that, and also knows that deep down, despite my love for him, the man now sitting beside me will always hold a special place in my heart.

My body too. I had almost given my maidenhood to Andrew.

He slowly peeled the scarf from my eyes. I squinted, trying to adjust to the sudden brightness. I had not seen Andrew in what seemed like years, and here he sat beside me looking as handsome as ever with his dark wavy hair, deep blue eyes, and the infamous Hathaway cleft in his chin.

"I cannot believe that William selected you."

"Are you disappointed?"

I shook my head. "Quite the opposite. You know the whole story, I assume?"

"That your husband is impotent and you need to produce an heir, yes."

"And that two other men will also bed me?"

He nodded.

"Oh, Andrew…"

I hugged him, relieved that my first experience outside of my marriage would be with him. How I'd dreamed of him making love to me and yes, planting his seed inside me too.

"William has instructed me to make this as sexually adventurous for you as I can."

Heat rose in my cheeks and fear overtook my thoughts. What if I enjoyed it so much that I would not want to return to William, or began hating him for his inadequacy in the bedroom? No, I was loyal to him no matter what my body craved.

"Perhaps we can begin with me blindfolding you again and exploring your body here in the carriage."

I swallowed. It sounded delightful. "But the driver, what if…"

Andrew put his head out of the carriage window and called to the driver.

"You can leave the carriage here, walk back to the house, warm yourself by the fire in the kitchen for a few hours, and then come back and take the horse into the stables. Lady Langtry won't need to return to her home until later this afternoon."

"Yes, sir."

Andrew lifted the scarf from his lap and placed it around my head once more. He kissed me on the cheek and then the lips. We had embraced many times before but now it felt different. More urgent…yes, a prelude to sex.

"Do not think of William at all, as he does not wish you to be inhibited today," said Andrew.

I opened my mouth, allowing him to slip his tongue inside. It dueled with mine for a few seconds before he pulled away.

"You always had the softest and most beautiful skin of any woman I've ever known."

I drew in my breath when he ran his finger over the skin around my neck and collarbone. He pulled the shawl from my shoulder before planting tiny kisses across it. He moved to my breasts and kissed the tops of them. My nipples pulled and ached, causing them to become suddenly tender against the inside of my petticoat. We had always been tempted to strip one another naked but had never had the courage to do it all those years ago.

"I have a confession to make," Andrew whispered in my ear. "I would lie awake at night and try to imagine what your breasts looked like, whether your nipples were light or dark pink, and what it would feel like to suckle on them."

His voice was deep, its level just above a whisper. Perhaps what I was about to say was unbecoming of a lady but I couldn't help myself.

Andrew had stirred something inside me that only he could satisfy now.

"Then unbutton my dress and find out. Suck my breasts like they will be the very last feast you will devour in this life."

I leaned back, my head against the cold leather of the carriage seat, hoping Andrew would do as I'd requested. I felt his legs press either side of mine and realized he was now straddling me.

He ran his hand over my breasts a few times before slowly pulling on the top button of my dress. Andrew had difficulty with it, which in away added to the fun and anticipation. Finally it popped open and he moved onto the next one. This time he had more success and then it was on to the third one. So slow but so thrilling…

Andrew slid his hand over my breasts after he'd undone each of the buttons. Now he had my petticoat to deal with. Tiny bows dotted down the front and then…

He tugged at the first one and I felt the material loosen and cool air pass over my skin. Another tug, another, and then he peeled away the muslin from my breasts.

"Oh dear god, I have never seen such beauty." I heard a thud directly in front of me and realized he'd gone to his knees on the carriage floor. "I'm not sure if I want to touch or suck them first. Such a dilemma for a man."

I didn't care which order he pleasured them in just as long as he did it soon. I pushed out my chest seconds before feeling his hands roam over them. Touching me like I was something he thought might break. Tiny passes of his fingers, hesitant at first and then, yes, oh so urgent.

"Dark pink and luscious," he said pulling on both of my nipples. I wiggled on the carriage seat as he pinched and twisted them.

"What do they feel like?" I asked him.

"Like tiny rosebuds about to come into bloom."

"Kiss my breasts."

"With pleasure."

His mouth moved immediately to the right one. I groaned but then felt somewhat guilty that it was Andrew's and not William's mouth causing my pussy to pull and ache right now.

Andrew's lips passed over the left breast barely touching the sensitive skin around my nipple. I raised my hands, pushed them up under each breast, and offered them to him.

"Suck them," I said.

In seconds his lips surrounded my right nipple. Oh dear god. My head hit the back of the carriage, as I leaned toward his face and pushed my breast out toward him, hoping he could take more of it into his mouth. I ran my hand through his hair, as he turned his attention to the left nipple. He sucked and licked, even bit it slightly before pulling it with the very tips of his teeth.

William.

I thought of him and how I wish he'd do the same when he pleasures my breasts. Would it be awful of me if I told him Andrew had bitten them and it had been erotic and fulfilling?

My juices began pumping from me, and I was sure the carriage seat was growing damper by the second.

"Andrew, are you hard yet?"

"My dear Gillian, a man cannot get any harder."

The mere thought of a cock hard and erect sent my blood pumping and pooling inside me. Soon, oh so soon it would be in my pussy.

"Stand up and let me feel you."

He stood and guided my hand to his crotch. A burst of juices sprang from me as I touched the firm outline of his cock through his pants. It had been so long for me. I took a deep breath, knowing I could not last much longer.

"Take me inside your house and up to your bedroom, where I want you to fuck me all day."

I pushed the scarf from my eyes, staring for the first time at the wonderful bulge in his pants and then up at his handsome face. He offered me his hand which would be the first step on my journey to sexual bliss.

Chapter Three

Andrew's home looked very much as it had the last time I'd been there. Not lavish by any means, but comfortable with its rugs and paintings and sculptures everywhere. No sign of a woman's touch anywhere.

He had remained a bachelor; why, I had no idea. Many a lady before and probably after me had cast their cap at him.

"What are you thinking?" he asked, as we made our way upstairs to his bedchamber.

"Why you never married. You would have made a fine husband...you still would. I mean, after all, you are young."

"I think you know the answer to that. My heart belongs to only one woman."

"I am sorry that..."

He got hold of my hand and squeezed it. "Shh, now, do not spoil things for us today. No thinking about the past and what might have been."

Andrew was right. It was all forgotten now, and we had this very special day together. He held open the door to his bedroom, and I stepped inside. It was the first time I had been in there. When we had courted this had been off-limits to me and now I was venturing into unknown territory. But of course, my husband had encouraged and approved of it.

A fire burned heartily on the left side of the room. Andrew's bed had four posts and was draped in a maroon-colored cloth. A painting of me that he'd commissioned shortly after we'd met hung on the wall opposite. I stood and looked at it, remembering sitting in his parents' garden while the artist sketched away. Andrew had stood behind him, smiling at what he saw on the easel.

"You still have it," I said.

"Of course, it's a prize belonging. I have even requested that I be buried with it."

"Oh, Andrew. I'm so sorry. I hope you realize that I had no alternative but to marry William; my parents…"

He rushed to my side and held me. "As long as he's been good and kind to you, and you've been happy with him, that's all that matters to me."

I pulled away. "I have, very…but I've often thought about you."

"When William arrived at the house last week I thought it was to tell me something had happened to you, that perhaps you had died… and my heart broke."

I brushed the side of his face with my hand.

"However, when he told me about his problem, and how he'd chosen me as one of the three men to make love to you, I thought it was actually I who'd died and gone to heaven. I truly believed that having you in my bed for even a day was my reward in the afterlife."

He kissed me, and I threw my arms around him. The feel of his hard cock pressing into my belly sent my blood pulsing around my entire body.

I slid my hand down until it rested on his crotch. I gave his cock a tight squeeze through his pants and he groaned.

"I want to feel you in my hand," I said.

I tugged at the bindings on his pants and opened them enough to sneak my hand inside.

Finally, there was my treat, hard and hot, long and thick. I gave it another squeeze.

"I want to suck it," I said.

"But Gillian, I'm supposed to be pleasuring you."

"Then I shall make this my first course."

I fell to my knees, pulling open the front of his pants until his cock was freed. I caught a glimpse of his balls too, and couldn't help but touch them and run my finger around each sac. They were so beautiful to behold.

"How I've dreamed of this very scenario for years," said Andrew.

"And how about this one?"

I lifted his cock and took him into my mouth, inch by delectable inch.

"Oh dear god. It's true isn't it? I have died," Andrew murmured.

I licked some moisture off its head and then slid my tongue along its underside. It was salty, hot and very delicious. I placed my hands upon his thighs and went to work on making him climax. Since William's illness I've been out of practice, and I hoped I hadn't lost any of the skills my husband first taught me on our wedding night.

Andrew began thrusting toward the back of my throat, as I sucked harder. I held his body tight, resting my hands on his ass cheeks, as he enjoyed his release and shouted out my name. I swallowed, enjoying the obvious pleasure I'd brought to him, hoping it could in some small way make up for me exiting his life so abruptly five years ago.

"I'm supposed to be filling your pussy, not your mouth, with my seed," he said.

I stood. "Like I said; a wonderful first course for me." I licked my lips.

"But now I have to grow hard again."

"Perhaps looking at my pussy will help with that."

* * * * *

I giggled as I turned and flopped down on his bed. My dress, where he'd not re-buttoned it completely in the carriage, fell open at the top. I tugged on the bows of my petticoat and let it fall open to expose my breasts again.

"You are aware that you are the most beautiful woman in the world," said Andrew. "Your husband is the luckiest man alive."

I leaned back on my elbows. "Do you want to check out my pussy to see if you find beauty in it too?"

"I most certainly do. But may I feel before I view it?"

That sounded, naughty, daring… "Of course."

He walked toward me. I lay back on the bed, feeling it sink slightly as he climbed upon it with me. My nipples stood erect and throbbed, as Andrew, not taking his eyes off me, pushed his hand up under my skirt and petticoats. His finger made a seductive march up my leg. It tickled and made my juices flow more as he inched his way toward my thigh. He ran two fingers over the top of my leg before making tiny circles up the rest of my thigh until he found my mound. He flicked his index finger over my pubic hair.

"I am guessing that this matches your beautiful dark tresses."

He buried his finger deep inside my curls and kissed me, as he drove deeper and found my clit.

"This feels as delightful as your nipples."

He made circles over and around it, as my pussy ached like never before.

I spread my legs, as Andrew pressed harder and rubbed my swollen nub. I murmured, already enjoying his touch and expertise.

"Make me come."

I leaned my head back, arched my back, and gave tiny thrusts upward creating friction between his finger and my clit.

Dear god…I felt suddenly on fire down there, as my legs bucked and I enjoyed my first climax not brought on by my own or my husband's hand.

Andrew kissed me again. "You come so very quickly," he whispered. "And look even more beautiful when you do…if that is possible."

"My pussy needs more attention now." I hope he didn't think I was desperate, but in a way I was. Although William touches my pussy, the thought that a cock would soon be filling it again made me brazen.

Andrew's finger slid down my folds and rested on the very edge of my slit. He teased me at first, pretending he was about to ease it inside me, but then didn't.

"Please, Andrew, do not make me wait." I ran my finger down the side of his face.

He laughed and then pushed his finger up inside me, making me take in a deep breath of air.

"You feel so wonderful; hot, wet, tight." He pushed farther up inside me and I closed my eyes, as his finger twisted around in there.

"Fuck me with your finger," I requested.

"It would be my pleasure."

I lay back and looked at the maroon cloth draped over the bed, as Andrew withdrew his finger then plunged it back inside me, repeating the delightful movement three more times until his middle finger joined the first.

The room appeared to spin as Andrew went deeper and harder, until I couldn't stand it any longer and had to squeeze my ass chees together to help my climax along. I swung my hips up off the bed, meeting his fingers, and that's all it took. I whimpered and shook, as Andrew leaned over and brushed his lips against mine.

"Your pussy feels so delicate. I want to see it now."

He helped me out of my dress and then pulled down my petticoat, eased my leggings off my feet, and pushed my legs apart.

I watched his reaction as he focused on the spot between my legs.

A tear appeared in his right eye.

"You are the most beautiful woman I have ever seen, Gillian. Your pussy is so luscious, so red."

What he did next took me by surprise. His got between my legs and licked my pussy and clit before plunging his tongue inside me and lapping at my juices. His tongue gently slipped inside me and flicked the very opening of my sex.

I became suddenly jealous, which I knew was stupid, but I wondered how he was such an expert at this and assumed he had been with many women since I'd left his life.

Andrew licked a complete circle around my slit before flicking his tongue over the entrance. I raised my ass. William often licks my pussy but had never made me feel like this: I felt I was slipping backwards into a warm, soft bath. I closed my eyes, knowing I was nearing bliss.

He flicked harder, wilder. It was too much for me, and I needed to find relief from this pleasant torture. I placed my arm over my eyes and let him bring me to climax yet again. I had enjoyed three already, but none of them yet had involved an act that would get me pregnant. William had sent me here for that very reason, so I couldn't let him down.

"Andrew, are you hard?"

"Would you like to see for yourself?"

I leaned back on my arms again, as he pulled down his pants. His very aroused cock sat up on his belly. It was bigger than William's, or at least bigger than I remembered it being when he was aroused.

Andrew pulled off his shirt and threw it on to the floor before easing his body on top of mine.

I pressed my finger onto the cleft in his chin. I always thought it so becoming.

"Are you ready for me to make love to you?" he asked.

"Of course, and I hope and pray that it will be your seed that makes an heir for my husband."

"I will do my best."

He nudged my leg with his right knee, and soon he was easing his cock into my slit.

I tensed up, probably because it had been such a long time since I'd been with a man, and couldn't help but flinch as his dick stretched my muscles almost to the point of pain. Andrew must have seen my discomfort.

"Gillian, have I hurt you?" He stopped penetrating me.

I shook my head. "It is just that it's been so long without William inside me."

"Then I will be a careful lover."

Andrew couldn't be anything else.

He pressed his cock to my entrance again, and this time gently slid inside me until he filled me. I was no longer in discomfort but sheer bliss.

I tightened my pussy as Andrew gently rocked his body back and forth over mine, sending his cock higher up inside me.

I held his arms and then made circles on his biceps, as my pussy clenched around his sex. I remembered that bringing my legs up and resting them on top of William's ass made him slide deeper, and helped me come with much more intensity. I hoped Andrew didn't mind me doing the same with him.

I crossed my legs at my ankles and rested them on his bottom.

Oh yes, that felt so wonderful, as his dick filled me and hit a sweet spot that I remember liking so much. "Fuck me harder."

He probably thought me demanding, but I needed my climax and wanted it soon. I'd waited so long for this, and here it was…

I braced myself, as I remembered the sensations I used to feel around my mound and anus when William was taking me over the edge.

I cried and screamed when my orgasm took me. I turned my headfirst to the right and then to the left, breathing deeper, wanting this to last but knowing it couldn't. And that's what made me cry.

And Andrew was panting heavily now, saying my name over and over again as he picked up intensity, until finally he went still, and his semen spurted inside me. He gently rested his body down upon mine with his cock still buried deep within me. He kissed me.

"I'm sure that I died in some horrible accident while I was riding my horse, and have gone to heaven, and you are my reward."

I pinched him, and he laughed. "You are still very much alive."

"And I must thank your husband for allowing me to make love to his beautiful wife."

I brushed the hair from his eyes. "When you are hard again I want you to make love to me once more."

Chapter Four

"So, do you pleasure yourself?"

Should a woman ever own up to doing such a thing? I took a deep breath. Of course when one's husband is impotent, the answer is absolutely. And seeing how Andrew was once a suitor, I had no problem admitting it.

"Yes, but I don't let William know about it."

"Why ever not?" He flicked my nipples as we chatted.

"He pleasures me with his fingers and I've told him it's all I really need."

"But it's not?"

I shook my head. "I find that I need more. Over these past few years I have, in fact, grown insatiable in the pleasure department. However, if William ever knew that he is not satisfying me fully he would be heartbroken, so whenever he's out hunting or riding I take to our bedchambers and touch myself."

He lifted my hand and kissed its palm.

"And is it always pleasurable?"

"Yes. Out of sheer necessity, I've become skilled in the fine art of masturbation."

"Then may I watch how you do it?"

I opened my mouth, ready to say absolutely not. I'd been embarrassed to even admit I do such a thing, and now to do it in front of...Andrew... I closed my eyes.

"Please, it would give me the greatest pleasure to see you touch yourself," he said. "In fact, all men like it. I'm sure William will not be upset to know that you masturbate."

"Andrew, please, you will not tell William that I do such a thing when his back is turned, will you?"

"Of course not. It will be our little secret. However, I know it would bring him great joy, as it will for me right now." He ran his finger over my nipple.

"As it's you, very well then."

Andrew turned on his side and rested his hand on his arm. He did not take his eyes off of me now.

"When I first learned to pleasure myself, I used to lie flat on my back and imagine William was fucking me."

"But now?" asked Andrew, running his hand between my breasts and onto my belly.

I got up onto my hands and knees. "I have found a better way to enjoy an orgasm brought on by my own hand."

"And how did you discover such a thing?"

"I dropped my hairbrush while I was naked, kneeled down to pick it up, and caught sight of my reflection in the mirror. I was so sad that my husband could no longer have an erection and how much I missed having him inside me. I was not sure why, but I put my hand down between my legs like this and started to feel and explore my body to see what brought me pleasure."

Andrew watched as I pushed my hand through my curls and circled my clit, rubbing harder on each passing. I lifted my head up, almost forgetting that Andrew was now a spectator. I slid my middle finger down onto the entrance of my pussy and circled it too. I was still very wet and hot from Andrew fucking me, so my orgasm crept up on me before I'd done much work on myself. My knees grew weak, my heartbeat faster as my finger slipped inside, and as I always did as this point; I imagined William thrusting hard inside me.

I cried out as my finger hit my sweet spot at the back of my quim, and my climax possessed me.

"Oh, Gillian, stay as you are."

Andrew got behind me, parted my ass cheeks and entered my pussy. I arched my back toward him, feeling his cock fill me, spreading my vaginal walls to their fullest as his thighs smacked into my bottom.

My nails dug into the bed cover, as he thrust so hard that he almost lifted me up in the air.

I hung my head down and sank my knees onto the quilt, as my pussy burned and pulsed and I enjoyed yet another glorious orgasm.

Glancing between my legs, I caught sight of the bottom half of Andrew's balls, as he drove his body against mine. He ran his hands over my back, as once again he cried my name, and warm liquid gushed inside me and then trickled down my legs.

He encouraged me to lie on the bed. He cradled me in his arms and brushed the hair from my eyes. Next he kissed me and traced the outline of his face with my fingers.

"You'll have to leave soon and return to William."

I loved my husband, but Andrew's announcement made my heart heavy.

He rubbed my belly. "Perhaps an heir for your husband is being conceived at this very moment," he said. I touched my belly as well.

I put my hand on top of his and pressed it down onto my womb, wondering what a child of mine and Andrew's would look like.

"Will you come and visit us soon?" I asked.

"I don't think that would be a very good idea, do you?"

He was right. I loved both him and my husband. And it wouldn't be fair to either of them.

I shook my head, as a tear slid from my eye.

* * * * *

William was waiting for me at the entryway when I arrived back later that day. He kissed the back of my hand and led me inside and up to our room. Once inside I threw my arms around him and kissed him.

"Thank you for selecting Andrew."

"So you and he had an enjoyable time together…I mean I hope that you and he…"

I nodded.

He took off my cloak and pulled me in close. "And I'm assuming you had an orgasm?"

"Many."

"Good, and Andrew is a fine lover…I take it."

I did not respond.

"You won't offend me if you say yes."

"Yes, he satisfied me."

"And I'm sure you him. He still loves you, you know. I gathered that when I visited him the other day. When I asked him to make love to you, well, I have never seen a man so happy in all my days."

I nodded, remembering the portrait of me on his wall and his request for it to be buried with him.

"And what was it like to have a cock inside you again?"

I turned away, pretending I hadn't heard.

William grabbed my arm. "Gillian, you cannot offend me. You're a woman who has needs."

"It was wonderful."

He pulled me close and rubbed his face against my hair. "I can smell him on you. His cologne. It's very distinctive."

"Oh William, I should have bathed immediately upon."

"Nonsense. Now let me see your body and how it looks after a day of pleasuring."

I felt tired and wanted to sleep, but I could not deny my husband seeing me naked. I stripped off my clothing. William ran the back of his hands over my breasts. I closed my eyes, remembering Andrew's hands upon me, but tried not to think about it.

William lifted me up and carried me to the bed, where he sat me down and pulled my legs apart.

"So red and swollen now here." He pushed two fingers inside me, and I flinched.

"Oh, my darling. I've hurt you." He stood and kissed the top of my head.

"No, it's just my pussy is out of practice and a little sore, that is all."

He kissed my head again.

"William, slide your cock over my slit."

I thought he'd deny my request, but instead he opened his pants and flicked out his dick. I lifted my bottom as he got hold of his cock and slid it down my folds, brushing my slit with its head almost pushing inside me.

"That feels so wonderful," I said.

"You are a sweet girl, and don't feel guilty over what you did this afternoon. By the look of your pussy and the way you flinched, Andrew is a fine lover, and you had a good fuck."

I took a deep breath, my eyes heavy and almost fluttering shut.

"Now I think you should get some rest, because tomorrow another sexual adventure awaits you, my lady."

BOOK TWO-THE HIGHWAYMAN

Chapter One

I couldn't imagine what William had in store for me next. My body, but especially my pussy, were both in a state of arousal since my day with Andrew. I wondered who gentlemen number two would be and if my encounter with him would be just as exciting and, yes, physically thrilling too.

Once again, William led me out to the carriage in the morning and sat on the seat beside me, but this time did not blindfold me.

He took my hand and sandwiched it between his. "I need to give you instructions for today."

My heart skipped a beat. Perhaps sucking cocks would be off limits now. Yes, he'd given me permission to do just that, but I had not revealed that I'd done so with Andrew. Maybe he had sensed I had and was now having regrets. I turned to look at him.

"Remember when we were first married and we spoke of the fantasies we would live out once I returned from India?"

It had been so long ago that I'd almost forgotten, but now that William had reminded me… I coughed, almost embarrassed at recalling what I'd revealed to my then new husband.

"You wanted me to pose as a roguish highwayman who would stop your carriage and seduce you, and let's not forget have my wicked way with you."

"Yes, I remember."

"We never got to do that, because well, you know why, but I thought, 'What if my darling girl can live out her fantasy with another man?'"

I attempted to speak to tell him it would just not be the same without him posing as the man in question.

"Today, a highwayman will stop this carriage, and you are to role play and live out your wildest fantasy with him."

He exited before I could tell him I just didn't think I was brazen enough to do that sort of thing with a man I wasn't already intimate with.

However, he'd closed the door and ordered the driver on his way. I looked out to see William heading back toward the house. He must have sensed that I was watching, because he turned, waved, and blew me a kiss. How had I gotten so lucky as to marry a man who cared about me and my sexual needs as much as he did?

I slid back on the carriage seat and set my head against the leather headrest, wondering when and where the highwayman would strike. It was a beautiful day outside. The sun was shining, birds were singing, and

I was on my way to…well, the unknown.

The steady rhythm of the coach rocking from side to side relaxed me, so I shut my eyes, not realizing I'd dozed off until the carriage came to an abrupt stop.

Looking outside, I noticed we were on a side road with woods lining both its edges. The sound of a horse's hooves echoed in the distance and gradually got louder. A few minutes later, I heard a man's voice instruct the driver to get down from his seat and walk away.

My heart beat faster, hoping this was all part of William's game and not a real robbery. I jumped when suddenly a man with a black scarf tied around his face peered in through the window at me. I looked into his eyes, hoping I could tell his identity, but it was impossible.

"Miss, good day to you."

I nodded to him, hoping he wasn't a real highwayman. He opened the door and climbed inside the carriage.

"That's a beautiful necklace you're wearing."

I fingered the pearls William had suggested I wear.

"I'd like you to remove the necklace and hand it over to me."

I swallowed, thinking that perhaps this was a real highwayman. I reached behind my neck, unclasped the hook, and handed them over.

"Thank you. They will come in very useful later. And now, miss, I must ask that you take off all your clothing for me."

I sighed in relief. It was exactly the wording I'd told to William years ago when I'd revealed my wish and we had told one another what we would say during our fantasy. Despite this being a game, I had to put up some opposition for the fantasy to seem real…and pleasurable. "And what if I say no?" I asked.

"Then, miss, I will have to do it for you, and I shall more than likely rip some of your finery in my urgency to ravish you."

"I see. Then I should probably disrobe to save my clothing."

He slid onto the seat opposite me as I began to unbutton the top of my bodice.

The highway rogue lifted up a riding crop and laid it over his lap.

"Nice and slowly. Make me anticipate what fine body awaits my eyes."

I still couldn't place the voice, but he had a rich, deep timbre that made my pussy wet just thinking about him fucking me once I was naked.

After peeling back the top of my dress, I got to work on the bows on my petticoat. He raised his legs, placed his feet on the seat next to me, and crossed his arms. I pulled on the last of the bows on my top, and it fell open. Obviously not enough for his liking, because he took the riding crop and pushed away both sides of the bodice to reveal my breasts.

"Very nice; such large, pink titties." He gently grazed them with the end of the crop. They pebbled, and a gush of cream slipped from inside me.

I eased the dress and petticoat off my shoulder, letting them rest on my waist while he studied me. My hands shook now…not from nerves but anticipation of what would come next. I pulled the dress down over my hips and stood, pushing it down my legs until it fell onto the carriage floor. While I was standing, I decided to remove the rest of my petticoat. It too fell to the floor, and now I stood in front of the mystery man in just my shoes and leggings.

He ran the crop around the bows on each of their tops .I looked down, ready to remove them, when he stopped me by placing the crop on the back of my right hand.

"I like the look of you naked in nothing but your stockings. Step toward me a little so I can check you out more thoroughly to see if I've struck gold by stopping your carriage today."

He looked at me from top to toe. "Are you a virgin?"

I remembered I'd told William that I would play the innocent maiden who had never been touched by a man. "Yes, yes, of course I am."

"Well then, I can see I'll have some fun taking your maidenhead. Spread your legs for me."

I knew when I did he would probably see the wetness on the tops of my inner thighs. The flow was getting heavier with each word he spoke. I separated my legs, glancing down to see my cream glistening on my skin, but I wasn't ashamed.

He lifted the crop and ran it lightly over my belly, barely coming in contact with my skin. He passed it over my curls, then down into them. The end of the crop bit into my clit, and I shuddered not from discomfort but sheer pleasure.

"I think the lady likes that."

I wiggled my folds over it, hoping he would take that as a hint and also get his answer. He pulled it back and forth, scraping my clit until I could feel it engorge and throb. I had never been pleasured by anything inanimate before and had to admit, it was sheer bliss. I dug my feet into the carriage floor, curled up my toes, and had my first orgasm of the day on its fifth pass. I'd tried not to call out, but no one was around, so I went all out. I held the carriage wall to steady myself, because my legs convulsed from the excitement.

He burst out laughing. "I can see that you will be easy to please. Now turn around so I can inspect your ass."

Still on shaky legs, I slowly spun around. He nudged both my cheeks with the crop before running it down my crack. It tickled me, but I tried not to laugh.

"Very nice little bottom."

He gave it a sight slap with the stick, and I closed my eyes, shocked at how much I liked the feel of it on my buttocks.

"Bend over and put your hands on the carriage seat so I can get a view of your pussy."

I leaned over and drew in my breath as he ran the crop down between my ass cheeks and parted my pussy lips with it. I knew my cream was bubbling from me, because I could feel it. He had to know how excited I was about this game we were playing.

"Just as pretty and pink as your tits. Looking at your quim, I think you might be lying about being a virgin, so I think I should check before I fuck you. After all, I only make love to women who have never been touched before."

I braced myself, sensing what he was about to do to me. I took a deep breath, feeling as two of his fingers slipped inside me and pressed upward.

"Feels like no man has been here before, but it does seem like you're more than ready to lose your virginity. I have never known a maiden be this wet. It's as if you know what bliss lies ahead for you."

"No, it's because you excite me, sir, with your mask and deep voice."

He laughed and withdrew his fingers. "So are you ready for me to fuck you and take your maidenhead?"

"If you really must, then I assume I will have to accept it."

"Turn around."

I thought perhaps I would see his face now, but he kept it covered, which I have to say added to the thrill of this charade.

"Have you ever seen a cock before?"

I shook my head, loving this game more by the second.

"Then you are about to see your first one."

I glanced down, licking my lips as he unbuttoned his pants and pulled it out. His dick sprung up on his belly, its veins standing out due to its hardness.

"You're looking as if you want to touch it, do you?"

I didn't respond but instead reached out and caressed it. It was hot with pre-cum oozing slightly from its slit.

"I can assure you it will only hurt for a few minutes, and then there will be just sheer pleasure when I'm inside you."

He threw his coat onto the carriage floor behind me. "Now lie down and relax as best you can."

I crouched down on the floor and rested my body on the coat as the mystery man got down there with me. It was a tight fit in the carriage, but it made it all the more exciting.

He lifted my legs by their ankles, parted my legs, and rested my heels on both seats of the carriage so I was open wide to him.

His cock was hot, almost smoldering, as it penetrated me.

"How do you like a man's cock inside you, my dear girl?" he whispered.

"It's not like I ever expected."

"And probably neither is this."

He penetrated me more, hitting the back of my vagina as I put my legs around his hips and arched up to meet his first thrust.

Dear god, he knew how to fuck a woman which had me all the more puzzled as to who he was. I dug my nails into his arm as he fucked hard and fast.

"That is it, my dear, enjoy and love it as I am savoring every second of fucking you," he shouted.

The pleasure in my pussy was almost too much now. I wanted him to slow down, but then again, didn't want him to. I lifted my hips with all my strength, feeling his cock fill me more. I placed my ankles back on both seats and used them to leverage myself upward as I felt my climax drawing close.

"Fuck me, fuck me harder," I shouted.

"Is that the way for a virgin to talk, you naughty girl? But if you insist."

I screamed out from pleasure and not pain. I almost lost consciousness as he drove hard and sent me into a sheer frenzy as I climaxed. I cried, because I felt so wonderful inside. I shuddered, went still, and then realized he was now spilling his seed inside me.

"Well, now, miss, I've not only taken your necklace but your maidenhead too."

"I should report you, but I've no idea who you are."

"Do you want to?"

"I want to at least see the face of the man who has taken my innocence."

"Then pull away the scarf from my face."

I lifted my hand and tugged at it until first his nose was displayed and then…

I knew I'd turned red when I saw who it was, because my cheeks felt suddenly flushed. He was William's best friend, James Horton, who had gone to India with him and not left his side during his illness there, and on his return to England. Every night he had sat with me, helping to tend him and sometimes watching over him while I rested.

"You are blushing, dear Gillian. There is no need for that. William has told me everything. I never knew his illness had caused such a disaster for the two of you."

His shirt tickled my nipple, and at that very moment I wanted him to touch me, fuck me again.

"What is it, Gillian?"

"Nothing."

"Now, tell me." He lifted my chin so I had to look at him in the eye.

"I have enjoyed this so much that…"

"You would like more fun and games?" asked James.

"But now…"

"You know who I am you're embarrassed."

I nodded.

He kissed me and pinched my nipple. "You are so beautiful and a pleasure to make love to. This carriage is on my property, and there is a small hunting cottage just a short walk through the trees. How about we go there so I can seduce you some more? I am sure William would approve."

I sat up, hoping he didn't see how eager I was. He wrapped his jacket around me and carried my dress and petticoat and led me through the trees. The cottage was a few feet ahead of us, and I felt excited to get inside there so I could be fucked again.

Once inside, I threw James' coat off my shoulders and slipped my shoes and leggings off and threw them onto a nearby chair. James grabbed me and pulled me into his body. My hand slipped down onto his crotch.

He was hard again.

"You are a naughty highwayman."

I pulled at his shirt until all the buttons flew off and at various spots around the room. His hair-covered chest was so inviting, because William is lacking in that department. I put my face onto it and took in his scent. Sandalwood, soap, so intoxicating. My hand went to his cock, and I gave it two quick, but nevertheless hard squeezes.

"Does the lady wish to be fucked again?"

"Oh yes, the lady does."

I ripped his pants open more and pushed my hand inside, feeling not only his cock but his balls too. I ran my hand over each one, feeling James groan. He kissed me, and I playfully bit his lower lip before pulling it between my teeth. James ran his hands all over my ass before slapping my left buttock. I giggled before we kissed again. He pulled away.

"Go and sit in that chair for me."

I turned around to see where he was pointing. It was an armchair with both high back and arms. I walked over to it and sat. James was right in front of it now. He kneeled and lifted my legs up and spread me open before resting them on both the chair's arms. He glanced down between my legs, then up to my face.

"My dear girl, what torture it must be for poor William to see such beauty between your legs and not being able to plunder into it."

He opened my labia with his thumb and index finger and made a tiny circle at the very entrance of my slit with his middle finger. I sucked in my breath.

"And what absolute hell for you not being pleasured by your husband's cock."

"You can make up for it right now," I whispered.

"And I intend to for not only you but my best friend too."

I sat my head back against the high back of the chair when his mouth went on my folds and began to suck me. His teeth grazed my clit before his tongue plunged deep inside me. He flicked it so quickly I wondered where he'd learned to do such a thing. I had seen James with only a handful of women, but he had never shown an interest in taking a wife. I slid my fingers through the waves of his hair, pulling at the curls around the nape of his neck, and fingered his strawberry-shaped birthmark as he brought me closer to the edge of ecstasy.

He playfully bit me, then plunged hard and deep. I threw my hands in the air and held the back of the chair, lifting my buttocks to offer him more of my pussy. His tongue slipped higher, and that was all it took.

I cried out, positive that people from miles around, even William, had heard my screams of delight.

I watched my juices flow from my pussy and literally drip onto the chair beneath me.

James reached up and grabbed both my nipples and pulled, ending them into as big a frenzy as my pussy. He placed his hand over both my breasts and squeezed.

"Such beauty, like fine works of art."

He squeezed again before reaching into his pocket for my pearl necklace.

"Are you going to put them back around my neck?" I asked.

"No, not yet, because I have something better to do with them."

He held them in his palm as he reached up and massaged them over my breasts. I couldn't believe how something so simple could feel so wonderful as the beads slid over my skin. I rested my head back on the chair as he passed them over my nipples, then down my belly.

"Look how beautiful the opaque beads look against your dark curls."

I glanced down, seeing him running them over my pubic hair. He was right; the contrast of colors was stunning. I gasped when he wrapped them several times around his hand and began pressing them into my folds. A few beads bit into my clit, causing me to whimper.

"Does that feel good, Gillian?"

"Feels like heaven." I could hardly get the words out as he slid them lower, letting them scrape my slit. They were slippery, slightly cold, and I threw my head back as he pushed them up inside my pussy.

"I'm going to watch you come this time," he said.

He rubbed the beads back and forth, each time letting one or two of them slip inside me and brush against the opening to my quim. I held the sides of the chair and dug my nails into it. My nipples tingled, my belly and womb pulled, as James didn't take his gaze off me.

I mumbled something that was even inaudible to my own ears.

James moved his hand with increased speed and pressed hard. My heartbeat faster, my breathing… Well, his actions were almost taking that away. I inhaled and couldn't hold off any longer. I came, screamed, and felt juices almost spurt out of me onto James' fist.

"You are very stunning when you come. Your eyes become larger, that delightful, little mouth turns upward."

"I want to do something for you now."

"Oh, I think you already have."

"Stand up and drop your pants for me."

He did as I asked, and soon his trousers were on the ground, and I was now looking at a beautiful cock sitting on his belly. I stroked it, and it was his turn to draw in his breath.

"Change places with me," I suggested.

I stood and let him sit in the chair. I kneeled in front of him and ran my hand down his chest, loving the feel of his chest hair under my fingertips. I took my index finger and slid it seductively as I could down the middle of his belly and the line of hair that went down toward his bellybutton. His cock sat up close to it, his thick, pubic hair highlighting it.

I ran my finger down his shaft, seeing him grip the arms of the chair in very much the same way I had just minutes earlier. A bead of pre-cum bubbled from the top.

Deciding I wanted to experience all of James, I leaned into his body and kissed his cock before taking its top into my mouth. He placed his hand on the top of my head.

"Do you think this will be all right with William?" he asked.

I pulled away from him. "He has given his permission."

James nodded as I leaned over and took him into my mouth inch by inch, feeling his cock hit the back of my mouth. I licked and sucked as

William had taught me when we were first married. I felt James' feet fidgeting by my leg, and every so often he was beginning to mumble.

"Oh, dear Gillian, William is such a lucky man."

I took more of him into my mouth and let all my inhibitions leave my mind. I slid one of my hands down my thighs, finding my folds, and rubbed my clit as I sucked on James. He lifted his butt and began tiny thrusts inside my mouth, exciting me so much that I went all out on my clit, almost biting his shaft when I brought myself to climax.

I kept sucking as he moaned, groaned, and exploded into my mouth as I swallowed several times, taking in his salty seed.

He looked down at me, I up to him.

"William has been a good teacher," he said.

I nodded. "The best."

"However, we need to get you pregnant."

I had almost forgotten the real reason I was here with James.

James stood, his cock already surprisingly hard and high on his belly. "Come, let's head to the bedroom."

He offered me his hand, which I took, and I followed him to another room where a bed sat against the wall. I took the initiative and hoped James didn't mind that I was a lady who did exactly what she wanted in the bedroom. I pushed him down flat on the mattress. I go tonto it as well and ran my hands down his belly until it found his cock. It was a beauty, entirely smooth apart from the lovely veins that stood out from its skin, the slit still glistening from his earlier orgasm.

I couldn't control myself. I pushed my legs over his thighs and straddled him before raising myself up and brushing my folds and slit over the very tip of his cock.

Suddenly I felt ashamed that I'd never done this with my own husband, but William had after all given me permission to do what I wanted. I impaled myself down onto his dick. It was the most beautiful feeling in the world as not a minute space was to be had inside me. I moved on him like I'd been taught when they'd first put me on a horse as a young girl. James moaned and lifted his buttocks to help me as I rode him fast and hard. I played with my tits as the zing in my pussy grew urgent. Pleasure pulsated into my thighs and ass and pulled hard on my nipples, and I loved looking at James' face as he watched me. He smiled, obviously enjoying this as much as me.

I raised my arms, lifted my ass up and down to bring about my climax. It weakened me, because it was so all embracing. I fell onto the bed, on my side, hoping my breathing and heartbeat would return to normal very soon. James ran his hands down my thighs and was inside me again. Not that I was complaining.

"I want to make sure William gets his heir. I feel I owe him that," he whispered in my ear.

James drove hard into me until he climaxed and filled me. The mix of my juices and his seed streamed down my legs. He turned me over and kissed me while playing with my tits. He flicked them, then seductively circled them with his middle finger.

"Why have you never married, James?" I reached up and wiped away some sweat from his brow.

"I suppose I have never found the right woman."

"Will it upset you when you come to visit us now and see a child that perhaps could be your own son or daughter?"

He shook his head. "I will think of it as a gift I have given to my very best friend and his beautiful wife. The thought of my child growing in your womb excites me so."

He ran his hand over my belly, and I held it there.

"I blame myself for all this trouble as I'm the one who talked William into going to India with me. Had I not, he would not have fallen sick and become impotent."

"You know I should have guessed there would be some connection to you when he insisted I wear the pearls this morning. He purchased them for me before you set sail."

"Ah yes, the pearls. He mentioned he would make you wear them and I was to use them to pleasure you."

"And you certainly did."

"May I pleasure you again with them?"

Just thinking about that made my pussy slick and hot again. "I would very much like that."

He got up and left the room, returning with the pearls dangling over his hand.

James sat next to me on the bed and ran the tiny beads all over my body, over my breasts, my nipples, and thighs.

I laid back and relaxed. He pushed them down into my curls and rolled them around my folds.

"My husband thought of this. He is such a clever man," I said, almost giggling with the sensation the tiny beads were causing.

"And there is more. Get up on your hands and knees."

I couldn't wait to see what was in store for me next.

"Hold the one end of the necklace through here."

He pushed my legs apart and handed me the clasp. I grabbed it with my right hand.

"Are you ready, Gillian?"

"I would be if I knew what I was ready for."

He pulled the necklace upward into my folds as he pulled one way, and I realized I was supposed to pull the other.

Dear god, how had William thought of such an erotic act using my necklace of all things? The beads grazed my slit, and then two went inside me as James pulled. I pulled back, throwing my head up like a rearing horse. I took a deep breath, pulled hard; James snatched them, and that's all it took. I fell face down on the bed, panting as my pussy literally shook.

James rubbed my ass before smacking it.

"I will have to thank my husband for this, that is if I recover enough to go home today," I muttered into the quilt on the bed.

I rested my head on my hands as James rubbed his hands all over my ass and lower back. He kissed the nape of my neck before dragging his tongue along the path of my spine.

"So are you James now or the highwayman?"

"Which one do you want me to be?" he whispered close to my ear.

His breath tickled my ear.

"James is exciting, but the highwayman knows how to fuck a lady."

"And how would an innocent virgin like yourself know that?"

We both laughed, and he slapped my buttocks again.

"Unless of course the lady lied."

"So, highwayman, am I the best female you've ever fucked?"

He ran his finger down my crack. "I'm not quite sure, because it's between you and the lady I seduced just last week. Stopped her carriage between here and London."

"Really."

His finger penetrated my pussy, and I wiggled my ass.

"Of course we could settle this by me fucking you again so I could tell for sure who's the best one."

"That sounds fair enough."

"So do you prefer me to fuck you on your belly or back?"

"I think my back."

He rolled me over, lifted my legs, and parted them. I watched with utter delight as he held his cock and slipped it inside me again.

"Oh yes, have to say, your pussy is much tighter than the previous lady's."

I held his arms as he drove into me, moving the bedcover as he pushed hard and deep. I lifted my legs and butt, hoping to set up my resistance to James. I set my head back, pushing my chin up into the air as my juices flowed and my pussy gripped James' cock as my climax grew closer.

Taking a deep breath, I gripped the bedcovers and screamed out

James' name as I enjoyed my orgasm. Suddenly I felt guilty that it had not been William's name I'd hollered. James went still, called my name, and caused me more guilt as his seed filled me.

He pulled out and set his body next to mine. I shouldn't have, but I rolled over and snuggled into him, suddenly wanting him to comfort me and to ask forgiveness for enjoying myself a little too much today.

"You are the best lady of them all," said James, pulling me close.

"And what if you have gotten me in the family way today?"

"Then I shall do the decent thing and marry you."

His humor lightened my sudden dark mood.

"I shall sleep well tonight with all this physical activity," said

James.

"Me too."

"And I suppose we should get you dressed, find the carriage driver, and send you back to your husband."

"Thank you, James, thank you so much for today."

"It's been my pleasure."

* * * * *

William had the servants draw a bath for me as soon as I arrived home. I got undressed, and he held my hand as I stepped into the warm, lavender-scented water. It felt wonderful as I pushed my shoulders down under its welcoming warmth.

He sat down beside the bath, cupped some water in his hand, and let it dribble down over my chest.

"Here, lean forward so I can wash your back."

I did as he asked, and he circled my back with a sponge and soap.

"Did you have fun today, my darling?"

"Yes, James is…"

"You can say it. I've told you before you will not hurt me."

"He is an entertaining lover and a splendid highwayman."

"I thought he would be. He's always been adventurous, so I guessed the bedroom would be no exception."

"He took my innocence, you know." I almost giggled.

William laughed. "Perhaps I should challenge him to a duel."

"He has promised to marry me if I am with child."

William laughed again and put his hand down in the water and on my stomach.

"I think you will look beautiful with a growing belly."

He leaned over and kissed me.

"May I feel your pussy?" he whispered.

"William, you're my husband; you don't need to ask such a thing.

It is your right to touch me."

I took his hand, lowered it through the water, and placed it between my legs.

He pushed his finger inside me. I was sore after today's lovemaking with James but didn't have the heart to tell him. I hoped he didn't see me suck in my breath.

"At least this work of art has enjoyed some activity. May I bring you to orgasm?"

"Dear husband, it is a requirement."

BOOK THREE-THE RAKE

Chapter One

The following day I was prepared for William to once again lead me outside and put me in the carriage, but he did not.

"In case you're wondering, my dear, your next adventure doesn't begin until later this evening."

"And where will I be heading?"

"Not very far this time. In fact, just up the stairs to our bedroom."

I knitted my eyebrows together and looked at him. He had a devilish grin on his face that I thought was quite becoming.

"The gentleman will be calling upon you in our bedchambers," he finally said.

"William, what if he is seen… What if he is heard pleasuring me?"

"Do not worry about that. I will be there too and any noise you make, any whimpers of delight escaping that pretty mouth of yours, will be assumed by both my mother and the servants to be of my doing."

I coughed, not quite sure what to say, what to think of William's decision to bring a man into our home to…

"You would not say no to your husband having a little fun watching a man pleasure and fuck you, would you?"

Suddenly I didn't know the answer. Not that I'd deny my husband anything, but what if he saw the enjoyment I got from another man's body and was heartbroken? Or what if I was too inhibited to enjoy my orgasm?

What if I wasn't able to even reach a climax with William observing me?

He grabbed my hand, obviously seeing the apprehension written all over my face.

"Do not worry, darling wife. You are free to do what you want with this man, scream with ecstasy, suck his cock, whatever, and I will be thrilled to just watch you."

* * * * *

We'd eaten dinner with my mother-in-law who remarked that I had a rosy glow in my cheeks and could there be the slightest possibility that I was finally with child?

William had kicked me under the table and winked. He'd commented to his mother that there was always a remote possibility that

I'd provide him with an heir one of these days.

We'd enjoyed a game of cards and a glass of sherry with her, then excused ourselves and retired to the bedroom.

"I expect your final lover will arrive any minute," said William ,looking at the clock on the mantel.

My throat was dry and my stomach turned as William poured himself a brandy.

I paced the floor a few times, but then a tap on the French windows made me stop in my tracks.

"Ah, our man is right on time."

William walked to the glass door and opened it, and inside strolled none other than his cousin, Clive.

I sat down, hoping the bed was behind me. Clive, the rake of the family. Clive, the young man who had bedded almost every woman in Hampshire and the neighboring counties. And Clive, my husband's cousin, who was rumored by all the ladies in our social circle to have a cock that hangs all the way to his knees. William would be watching us make love. I swallowed, the bile suddenly rising in my throat. Just why had William chosen him?

"Come in, dear cousin. Can I get you a brandy?" asked William.

"Perhaps later, after I have pleasured Gillian. I don't want alcohol o affect my performance tonight."

Clive glanced in my direction. I knew he must have seen the redness in my cheeks because I could feel my skin burning despite being several feet away from the fire. He walked over to me, lifted my hand, and kissed the back of it.

"My dear Gillian, William tells me I need to get you pregnant as he's unable to…you know…" He slowly raised his middle finger into the air. "Now don't worry, because three women have claimed I fathered their children, so I'm pretty certain I'm in good working order in that department."

I looked at William, my cheeks flushed and hot.

"It is perfectly all right, Gillian. I thought perhaps the odds were our child would be of Langtry blood if we had Clive fuck you. He's an expert at it or so I've heard." He winked at his cousin and slapped him on the back.

"Never had a complaint from any of the ladies," said Clive.

William poured another brandy. I stood, paced over to him, snatched the glass, and downed it in one gulp.

Both men laughed. "I think the lady is nervous," said Clive.

"Gillian, just relax my dear; enjoy Clive's expertise and my watching you.

So, as Gillian and I are new to this sort of thing, Clive, please do tell us how to begin."

"Perhaps, William, you can sit by the fire and enjoy your drink while you watch me take off your wife's clothing."

I looked at my husband. William had a smile on his face, sheer bliss written all over it. He seemed to like the idea and, after all, this was his evening as much as my own so I didn't protest. William sat and sipped his brandy as Clive began unbuttoning my bodice.

"You ladies have so many buttons on these damn dresses," he said as he got halfway down my back.

"Ah, but that makes it all the more fun when you finally get them open," said William.

Clive parted the material and pushed it over my shoulders until it hung around my waist. He continued with the rest of the buttons and soon my dress sat around my ankles. I stepped out of it as he started undoing the bows on my petticoat. He plucked at each one and pushed away the muslin until the warmth from the fire I now stood beside heated my skin. I felt my cheeks heat even more when suddenly my petticoat joined my dress on the floor. I hadn't worn leggings tonight so now I was naked in front of William's cousin— who had probably seen more nude women than the average man, but nevertheless we were related, and right then that was all that concerned me.

He looked me up and down. I wondered how I compared to his other women. He pulled the comb from my hair, freeing it to fall loose down my back. I shook my head to encourage my locks to cascade around my shoulders. William loves that look the best and I wanted to please him tonight. Clive walked around me and looked me up and down again as

William glanced over at me again.

"William, I wasn't aware that your wife was such a beauty. Had I been, well...I might have fucked her before now."

"Now, now, dear cousin. I have seen you eye my wife many a time and yes, it's one of the reasons I thought I should supervise tonight."

Clive laughed. "Yes, I am going to enjoy myself. So, Gillian, let us not waste any time." He offered me his hand. I took it and at first I thought he would lead me to the bed but instead he walked me over to

William.

"Here—sit on your husband's lap and kiss him, and pretend I'm not even in the room."

William placed his glass of brandy on the floor beside the chair and then offered me his hand. I sat on his legs and put my arms around his neck. His jacket rubbed my nipples as he pulled me in close and kissed me. I opened my mouth, feeling his tongue slide over my teeth. I playfully bit his top lip. "I love you," I whispered.

"I know, my dear."

He rubbed the backs of his hands over my nipples, and how I wished he could get hard enough for just this one night.

Clive's hands were suddenly on my back, making tiny circles downwards. I hated to admit it but it felt wonderful. I kissed William again but then pulled away when Clive's hands moved to my bottom and massaged my skin.

"It's all right, Gillian; let Clive caress you and get to know your body."

I squeezed my husband's hands as Clive checked out my ass, running his hands over each cheek and then around to the front of my hips. He kissed the nape of my neck.

"Kiss your husband again," he said.

I leaned in and put my lips on William's as Clive ran his tongue down my spine and pinched my bottom before sliding his fingers into its crack. One finger grazed my opening and I pulled away from William.

"Don't worry, Gillian, just let your inhibitions flow away," said William, stroking my hair.

"She feels delightful," said Clive.

"Turn around, my darling, so Clive can see just how wonderful you are," whispered William.

He seemed to be enjoying this more than I'd thought so I did as he said, hoping he would find pleasure in our ménage and not live to regret it.

I spun around on his lap and faced Clive, who stroked my breasts and then began pulling and pinching my nipples. The pressure he used was hard, almost painful, but strangely enough it brought on a sudden throbbing in my womb. He rolled them and then pulled again and wetness formed between my legs, probably causing a damp spot on William's pants. Clive took the weight of my bosoms in his upturned hands as William kissed my neck. I rolled my head his way as Clive tugged once more at my nipples.

"You like that, my darling girl, don't you?" asked William.

I hated to admit it, but it was already feeling erotic.

Clive ran his hands over my belly and then down into my curls.

"Here, put your legs either side of mine so Clive can take a look at the treasure that lies between them," said William, taking hold of my right one.

It was almost as if the two men had orchestrated the evening as

Clive winked at William.

I slipped my other leg over my husband's. I leaned back onto

William as he cradled me.

"Now, let's see what we have here," said Clive.

He kneeled in front of us and looked between my legs. Suddenly I wanted to snap them shut and get up, telling them I couldn't go through with this, but I had to for William's sake. I shook in my husband's arms.

"There, there, Gillian, don't be afraid; Clive is here to bring you nothing but pleasure."

William reached around my body and spread my labia with his index finger and thumb, and cool air passed over my slit as he opened me up.

"Very delightful, and she is highly aroused already," said Clive, swiping his finger along my folds. He lifted his hand and in the candlelight I witnessed my juices glistening on his fingers.

"Are you, sweet girl?" asked William. "Remember, your body cannot lie. Does Clive excite you?"

It was true, he did, and despite my apprehension I was very aroused.

Clive circled my slit with his finger and probed me slightly, just pushing inside the very opening of my pussy. He spun his finger around and oh my, it felt wonderful already. I leaned my head back toward William while spreading my legs farther apart.

"We are going to bring you pleasure jointly," said William.

I didn't know quite how they were going to do that but then

William began rubbing my clit as Clive pushed his finger deep inside me.

"Your wife has a hot and tight pussy, Cousin. My favorite kind."

He slid his finger out and then in as William kissed my neck and applied more pressure to my clit. I squeezed my buttocks, feeling my juices slide out and onto Clive's hand.

I murmured and whimpered as the two of them worked on me…harder, faster. William nipped at my neck as Clive pushed his finger higher up inside me, tickling the sweet spot at the back of my sex. My legs twitched suddenly and I couldn't seem to control them.

"There, there, Gillian. Just relax, my darling, and enjoy this moment."

I set my head back on William's shoulder as he kissed my collarbone.

"Dear husband, I love you." I shuddered and climaxed.

Now I lay weak, unable to move an inch, my legs sprawled over William's, my toes scraping the floor. William held me with a tight grip, obviously sensing I was about to slip to the floor.

When I looked up again, Clive was taking off his shirt. "I can see that the lady will need a cock inside her and very soon. William, if you'd do the honor."

"Here my darling, come with me." William encouraged me to stand and got hold of my hand. He walked me over to the bed.

"Lie down, Gillian."

I did as he asked and he climbed on the bed with me. He kissed me and ran his hands over my belly and into my curls, plunging his finger inside me and twirling it around as Clive had just done.

"I love you, my darling," he whispered.

"I love you too," I managed to get out as another orgasm took me. I turned my head to see Clive standing beside our bed, now completely naked. I couldn't help but stare at his belly and the beautiful specimen that stood upon it. The rumors were obviously true about his prized member. Juices flowed heavily from me as I anticipated him introducing it to my body.

He climbed onto the bed with us and nudged my legs apart with his knee.

William ran his hand down my cheek and looked into my eyes as Clive pushed his cock inside me.

I flinched and whimpered, feeling myself being stretched like never before.

"My darling, just relax and enjoy Clive's wonderful cock."

William offered me his hand and I squeezed it as Clive pushed further and higher up into my pussy. It hurt slightly, the pressure now pushing onto my back passage, but I knew the pain would quickly pass and took a deep breath.

"I think I may have just gone to heaven," said Clive, running his hands over my breasts as he started to thrust inside me.

All I could now feel was pleasure, intense pleasure as Clive's cock hit every part of my sex. He moved not only up and down but also sideways as I started to cry with sheer bliss.

William kissed me as I brought my legs up over Clive's buttocks.

Dear god, I would pass out and a doctor would need to be called. I dug my nails into William's hand and he laughed as I threw my head back.

"Fuck her more, fuck her harder, she is on the way to ecstasy," said William.

"With pleasure," said Clive thrusting so hard I was convinced that he'd moved my body several feet up the bed.

"Oh my dear girl, you're about to climax, I see it in your eyes," said William.

He was right. My pussy was throbbing, my womb pulling like never before. Ripples of pleasure tore through my bottom and legs. Clive thrust into me like neither of the two other lovers my husband had chosen, and as I climaxed I cried out my husband's name. I gripped his hand and he covered my mouth with his as Clive's semen flowed into me.

"That, my dear, was sheer bliss," said Clive. He pulled out of my pussy and then rolled onto his back on the bed beside me.

"So how was it inside my wife?" asked William. "It has been so long since my cock's been there I've forgotten how delightful it can be."

"Dear cousin, her pussy is sheer delight. Warm, almost boiling hot , tight, and when she enjoys her orgasm it is like a strong man's hand shake gripping one's dick."

I rolled onto my side and into William's as he threw his arms around me.

I was on the point of tears… Poor William.

"You don't know how wonderful it was to see a cock slide into you and to hear, see, and yes, to feel though my hand, your pleasure."

I put my hand on his crotch and squeezed. "William, I feel a little hardness down here."

"I did not want to say anything but watching Clive and you together, well, I felt some stirrings."

"Why didn't you say anything?"

I tugged at the buttons on his pants, spread the material apart, pushed my hand inside, and started rubbing him.

"Darling, do not get your hopes up for me."

"Will I embarrass you in front of your cousin if I take your pants off?"

"No, not at all. I am sure my cousin has seen another cock before tonight."

"Of course I have. Yes, you go ahead, William; strip off if you must," said Clive.

He raised his buttocks off the bed and I tugged his pants down his legs.

"Ah, now this is even more of a ménage," said Clive. "How about you go to work on William, while I work on you?"

I looked at William and he nodded. I slowly ran my hand up and down his shaft as Clive rubbed my back, letting his hand slide down my buttocks and then into the crack. I leaned over and kissed William's cock that was partly standing up now, and it gave me an idea. I got on my knees, parted my legs, and swiped the top of his shaft backwards and forwards over my slit. It did little for him and he lay there looking at me with loving eyes. I took hold of it and tried to push it up inside me as

Clive kissed my spine.

"Gillian, let Clive pleasure you, please. And let me hold and watch you again. I am afraid this is about as hard as my cock can get."

Clive slapped my ass and before I could protest, they'd rolled me onto my belly and pulled my arms up in front of my face, and soon both men were touching and rubbing my body with their hands and lips. I closed my eyes and wiggled around on the quilt as one of them ran a finger down my crack, and then onto my anus, and tapped it.

I burst out laughing. I hadn't realized I was so ticklish when someone, and I believe it was Clive, ran something that felt like a feather up my legs, parted my cheeks, and teased my pussy with it.

"I will have to remember this next time I pleasure her," said William.

"Women adore feathers and not just for their bonnets; they find something about the feel of them on their pussies irresistible."

He pushed it slightly into my entrance and twirled it. I giggled some more as he slapped my ass again.

"Okay, my cock needs to go someplace," said Clive.

He straddled me before pinning my upper body to the bed and then slipping inside my sex. I spread my legs as best I could to allow him more access. As Clive began to thrust William rubbed my shoulders.

"Tell me, Cousin, what does it feel like to be inside my wife's pussy this time?"

"Like easing in and out of hot velvet. One of the best I've had the pleasure of fucking."

I reached for William's crotch, put my hand around his cock, and held it as Clive drove harder and deeper inside me. I gave my husband's dick a tight squeeze each time a ripple of pleasure went through my body, hoping he could sense my joy. It hardened slightly and I smiled.

"Fuck her harder," said William.

"Whatever you say, Cousin."

Clive went all out, shifting my body up the bed as I squeezed

William's cock and shouted out his name as I climaxed. I cried into the bed as Clive brought me not one, not two, but three orgasms before his seed spilled inside me, mixed with my own juices, and slid out of my body and onto my thigh.

I turned over and looked up at William.

"Are you happy, my dear?" he asked.

I reached up and touched his face. "I am, but you know I wish it could be your cock inside me, your seed filling me, your…"

He kissed me. "This is the next best thing, and the night is young."

Chapter Two

By midnight my initial inhibitions about William inviting his cousin into our bedroom had completely vanished. William had decided to get under the covers to relax and keep warm while he watched Clive and me continue our sexual liaison.

Clive sat down in the armchair and poured himself a brandy.

Sipping it, he indicated for me to come and sit on his lap which I did.

"I've always wondered what brandy-covered breasts taste like."

Before I could say anything he'd tipped the rest of the liquor over my chest.

William burst out laughing as Clive took hold of my right breast, lifted it toward his mouth, and began sucking my nipple. I ran my hand through his hair, thinking how it was the same color as my husband's.

Dark brown with almost-gold streaks here and there—the Langtry trademark.

"Taste good?" asked William.

"You should try it sometime. Most scrumptious little buds it's been my pleasure to suckle."

He flicked his tongue over the other nipple and then gripped it with his lips.

"And Gillian, what does it feel like?" asked William.

"Your cousin has a quick and delightful tongue."

"Quick definitely; delightful, well, that's questionable," said

William.

"Do you know what? This titty appetizer has made me hungry for some pussy," said Clive.

He dipped his finger in the glass and swiped what was left of the brandy on it, pulled it out, and spread the liquor over my folds before pushing some up inside my pussy.

"Okay, my dear cousin-in-law, sit on this chair with your legs spread for me."

I stood and we changed places. I sat and rested my thighs over the chair's arms, letting my feet dangle.

Clive kneeled and put his face between my legs. Soon he was licking every inch of my folds.

"My dear cousin, you never told me your wife had a brandy flavored pussy. How unique."

William laughed and leaned back on his pillow.

Clive's tongue drove into me and he lapped at my brandy-scented juices.

I murmured when I felt the first stirrings in my womb. I looked across at William, and smiled when I noticed his hand was now under the covers and in the region of his crotch. He pleasured himself as Clive sucked harder and I groaned.

I leaned my head back and let myself climax, calling out William's name as I did so.

"Oh, there is more, dear Gillian."

Clive lifted me off the chair and pushed me against the wall. He raised one of my legs up and plunged into me so hard and fast that I squealed with both delight and the suddenness of his urgency to fuck me.

"Now all I have is a view of your buttocks, cousin," said William.

"Perhaps your wife can cover them with her hands for you."

I laughed, slapped both of Clive's ass cheeks with my palms, and dug my fingers into his skin as he thrust so hard he lifted my foot off the ground.

"Gillian, I want to hear you moan more," said William. "After all, you must be enjoying this like never before."

I'd been holding back thinking it would offend William, but he thought just the opposite. I groaned and clung to Clive as he moved my ass up the wall.

I pulled his hair by a tuft on the top of his head.

"Fuck me so hard my ass leaves an imprint on the wall," I said.

William burst out laughing. "That's my girl."

Clive bit my neck, and thrust so hard I did in fact slide my bottom down the wall which in turn caused me to climax. I screamed, hoping I hadn't been too loud, but right then my pussy ached and throbbed and the ripples of my orgasm were still traveling through my lower body.

Clive thrust more but then went suddenly still, groaned, and filled me until his seed poured down my legs.

Clive walked away, poured himself another brandy, and wiped the sweat from his brow as I looked down to see the skin on my thighs glistening with my juices and his semen.

"Come here, my darling," said William.

I walked over to him. He lifted the covers and I slid in beside him.

"Anything happening down here?" I asked, squeezing his cock.

"More stirrings as I watched Clive fuck you against the wall.

Someone's going to have a sore ass tomorrow."

"Yes, me," said Clive. "Your wife digs her nails into one's skin when she comes." He yawned.

"Tired, my dear cousin? Has my wife exhausted even a rake like yourself?"

"All I need is a few hours of sleep and I'll be ready to ravish her again."

William indicated for him to get in bed with us.

I was now sandwiched between the two men as William blew out the candle by his bed.

"If you need a fuck in the night, I'm here," said Clive, slapping my ass.

* * * * *

I fell asleep with my head on William's shoulder, thinking I would sleep like a baby after the evening's activity, but I awoke in the middle of the night, restless. I tried to just lie there and look straight into the darkness so I didn't disturb either of the men, but just couldn't. I turned onto my other side. The full moon shone into the room despite the heavy curtains. I noticed the outline of Clive's cock under the sheet as it lay across his thigh. It had felt magnificent and wonderful inside me. The temptation to touch it, stroke it, see how quickly my hand could make Clive hard, was getting the better of me.

Clive stirred, inching my way. I swallowed. Surely neither my husband nor Clive would have any objection to me having some more fun.

I eased my hand under the sheet, inching it toward Clive's crotch. I circled the top of his cock with my index finger, and Clive twitched. Next I ran my finger down its edge; Clive murmured. Finally I got the courage to take it into my hand and slowly I moved my hand up and down. Clive had obviously been awake and just pretending to be sleeping.

"Gillian, that feels so wonderful. A little harder, please, and you might give some attention to my balls while you're down there. Most of the ladies seem to forget about those treasures."

I aimed straight for them, letting my fingers glide through his thick pubic hair, and gave them a playful squeeze.

"That's it, just what I like."

I flicked them and then returned my attention to his cock, running my hand up it, feeling it harden and begin to leak pre-cum.

"You want me to fuck you again?"

"Not without William's knowledge."

Clive reached across my pillows and nudged my husband awake.

"What…"

"Cousin, your wife has woken up in need of a good fuck but she wants your permission to do so."

"Gillian, it's perfectly all right."

"Here, why don't we try it this way? I'll turn sideways, Gillian will face me, and then you can get behind her and hold her while I pleasure her," said Clive.

I turned over onto my right side, William held me, and then Clive turned to face us and lifted my leg before wrapping it over his thigh.

"William, do you want to get her ready for me?"

"With pleasure."

While Clive leaned in and sucked my nipples, William slid his hand down my bottom and between my legs, and finger-fucked my pussy until my juices seeped out of me.

"She is wet and waiting," said William.

He kissed my neck as Clive eased his cock deep inside me, and I whimpered with sheer delight. He dug his hand into my thigh as he thrust hard, sending my head upward on the pillow as William whispered into my ear that he loved me.

"This is quite the pussy your wife has. Like a vise," said Clive.

William held onto to me as Clive pushed harder, making me lightheaded, my pussy on fire and throbbing.

"Oh she is about to come," said Clive. "I know her quim well enough now to know that. Almost crushing my poor dick."

"Okay, Gillian, just breathe; relax and enjoy it like never before,"

William whispered.

Clive plunged deeper into me and that's all it took for me to scream out as William kissed my neck.

"I do hope that did not wake Aunt Cecilia," said Clive, rolling onto his back. Both men burst into laughter.

I turned and cuddled into William, feeling happy, and wondering what my mother-in-law would think if she knew her nephew had been pleasuring me all night in hopes of providing her with a much-longed for grandchild.

Chapter Three

When I woke the following morning Clive had gone and William was awake and looking at me.

"Good morning, my darling. Did you sleep well?"

I sat up and yawned. "Yes, very well."

"Clive has gone downstairs to have breakfast with Mother."

"So she will know he stayed the night."

"Knowing Clive, I'm sure he came up with a suitable story as to his presence here so early in the morning."

"Thank you for the last three days," I said.

I kissed him.

He rolled over and cuddled me. "I hope it has made up for the years you have gone without—"

I put my finger over his mouth.

"So you have had a good time these last three days?"

"The very best. Well, the best they could be without you pleasuring me."

"I suppose now all we have to do is wait to see if you are indeed with child."

* * * * *

I was, but the ironic thing was that when we announced my pregnancy two days before William's brother's wedding, Nigel shared a secret with us.

"My dear ones, this is the most exciting thing I could hear. Not only because I will at last be an uncle but because it will take an enormous pressure off me and Felicity."

"Really?" asked William.

"Yes, she has voiced her opinion against having children because childbirth petrifies her. Her two sisters died giving birth, you see. I told her we must have at least one child because you and Gillian have not provided one and the family name will die off. When I tell her that she doesn't have to deal with pregnancy and childbirth now she will be thrilled. Oh, Gillian, this could not have come at a better time. Your pregnancy is almost like a wedding gift to us."

* * * * *

When my time came to give birth I began to share in Felicity's fear. I had been in labor for a good part of the day and into the night, and had finally asked the nursemaids to ask William to pay a visit to the bedchamber as my pain was too much for me to bear.

"William, I fear I am about to die in childbirth! It's my punishment for enjoying such carnal passions with three different men. And for not knowing which one fathered this child who is obviously refusing to leave my body."

I screamed as another pain took me. He wiped my brow and kissed my forehead.

"Nonsense, my darling. The doctor is on his way and soon this will all be nothing but a distant memory for you."

* * * * *

Two days later, our son suckled at my breast. I was the happiest woman in the world to finally have a child. I pulled the blanket away from his mouth. My heart beat faster when I saw his chin. A few minutes after he'd been born I'd noticed a strawberry-shaped mark on his shoulder, similar to the birthmark I'd seen on James's neck during our liaison, and assumed he was James's son. But then, after the nurse had washed the blood from the baby's head, I'd seen the distinctive gold streaks in his hair and thought I'd been wrong and that Clive had fathered him. But now, as I looked down and saw the cleft in his chin, I realized that my former suitor Andrew was without a doubt my son's father.

William stepped into the room and sat on the chair beside us. I tried to pull up the blanket, hoping to delay the inevitable…that William would know that his son was my former suitor's child.

He stopped me.

"It's perfectly all right, my dear. I have no problem in raising Andrew's son."

He kissed my cheek.

"You already knew?"

He nodded. "We knew the odds. I will spoil the boy like he is my own, and you too, for giving him to me."

"I don't see how you could spoil me any more than you already do."

"Oh, I can. In fact, once your body has recovered from Henry's birth I think we should see about making the three men permanent lovers for you."

"William, you don't mean that, surely."

He kissed me again. "I do, and perhaps James and Andrew will agree to let me watch them fuck you next time around. In fact, perhaps all four of us can entertain you at the very same time."

I coughed, imagining what that would be like, and how many orgasms I would enjoy.

"Oh, and I should add this time around it won't be for the purpose of you providing me with an heir…no, next time is just for your pleasure, and nothing more."

THE END

Vanessa Devereaux writes both erotica and erotic romances. Her other works include The Brazen Ladies trilogy, The Secret Fantasy Society trilogy, including the bestselling The Vampire's Seduction. She writes for Totally Bound, Cobblestone Press and Evernight Publishing, and her short stories have been featured in numerous anthologies including Vanilla Free Christmas and Just Vamps. Her latest bestsellers include Christmas With a Cowboy and Courted by a Cowboy. She also pens an ongoing paranormal series titled Perfect Pairings.

When she's not writing, she's tutoring authors and teaching workshops.

Find out more about Vanessa at www.vanessadevereaux.com